Scholastic Children's Books
An imprint of Scholastic Ltd
Euston House, 24 Eversholt Street, London, NW1 1DB, UK
Registered office: Westfield Road, Southam, Warwickshire, CV47 0RA
SCHOLASTIC and associated logos are trademarks and/or
registered trademarks of Scholastic Inc.

First published in the US by Scholastic Inc, 2017
First published in the UK by Scholastic Ltd, 2017

Text copyright © Lisa Ann Scott, 2017
Cover copyright © Ilias Arahovitis represented by Beehive Illustration, 2017
Inside illustrations by Heather Burns copyright © Scholastic Inc, 2017

Trade ISBN 978 1407 17997 1
Book Club ISBN 978 1407 17995 7

A CIP catalogue record for this book
is available from the British Library.

Printed by CPI Group (UK) Ltd, Croydon, CR0 4YY

Papers used by Scholastic Children's Books are made
from wood grown in sustainable forests.

1 3 5 7 9 10 8 6 4 2

This is a work of fiction. Names, characters, places, incidents
and dialogues are products of the author's imagination or are used
fictitiously. Any resemblance to actual people, living or dead,
events or locales is entirely coincidental.

www.scholastic.co.uk

★ ✦ ★

Lisa Ann Scott

# Enchanted Pony Academy

**All That Glitters**

SCHOLASTIC

To my wild, creative,
wonderful Riley.
Love you!

# Chapter One

"I don't belong here." Daisy shook her mane, backing away from the crowd of ponies waiting to climb the rainbow to the Enchanted Pony Academy.

Uniponies played in the field of flowers. A pegapony soared into the air and floated down on magnificent wings. Right behind them, the rainbow that appeared in the very same spot each year was shining brightly, rising into the clouds. Soon, it would form stairs for each rare pony to climb. *Will the stairs appear for me?* Daisy wondered.

A pack of horses with glimmering hooves galloped by. Clouds of sparkles swirled behind them. They were Glitter Ponies – magical ponies. Daisy kicked at a patch of dirt, but her own sparkly hooves only stirred up a bit of brown dust. Her hooves were shimmery like the others, but they had never made glitter.

That one fact had worried her for as long as she could remember. All her life the question had swirled in her mind – was she really, truly magical? She was about to find out.

Daisy's mother gave her an encouraging nudge with her nose. "If you can climb the steps to the academy, you belong there. Only Glitter Ponies can climb the stairs."

"But what if I can't?" Daisy asked. "I don't know my Glitter Gift." Not only were Glitter Ponies magical, each one was also born with a special talent. Daisy hadn't experienced a smidge of magic yet. "What if my hooves are just a mistake?"

Mother smiled. "Then you'll come back to the farm and live a long, happy life with us. But if you can climb those stairs, you'll live with royalty someday."

All Glitter Ponies were sent to the Enchanted Pony Academy to develop their magic and skills, preparing them for the day they became royal pets. In addition to the glitter, some ponies had other rare traits, like wings and horns, or coats and manes of bright, beautiful colours. Daisy's fur was a boring shade of pale pink.

When the princes and princesses and royal children of the hundred kingdoms turned nine, they got to choose a magical pony from the academy. It was a great honour. But for a pony like Daisy, it would be incredible.

She'd been born in a small barn in the country. Her family had never seen a trace of magic in any of their foals. All her life, Daisy had seen Glitter Ponies from around the world gather at this very spot. Living so close to the rainbow, she'd watched them climb away to the magical land where the academy had stood, safely hidden, for hundreds of years.

Now that she was four, it was finally Daisy's turn. But she hung her head. "No one's going to pick me if I can't make magic."

"Every pony born with sparkly hooves is magical," her father said.

She stomped her hoof on the ground. Another puff of plain old dust rose up. Daisy usually kept her disappointment about her hooves to herself. She even covered them up with dirt sometimes so she could forget about them. But it was hard to escape her brothers' taunts and teasing about her useless hooves. How they would laugh if she was sent home! Today they stood nervously beside her, saying nothing.

"The academy will help you find your magic. Not everyone knows what their Glitter Gift is yet," Mother said. "We're so proud. We've been waiting for this day since you were born and we saw those hooves."

Mother had taught Daisy to read from a very young age, just so she could study every book in the library on the Enchanted Pony Academy. She could spend hours getting lost in the fascinating stories and history of the academy. But the longer her hooves stayed glitter-less, and the more time passed

without a gift, the more afraid she grew to even dream of this day, knowing she might not make it up that rainbow.

Now that the day was here, she wanted to be magical more than anything.

A trumpet sounded and the ponies started lining up in front of the rainbow. Daisy froze.

"Maybe the academy will let you wait until next year," her father said. "Since your magic hasn't appeared yet," he added softly.

Daisy swallowed the giant lump in her throat and thought for a moment. It would be easy to run back home. But she had to find out if she was magical. She had to climb those stairs. "I need to try, don't I?"

"That's my girl," Mother said.

Her brothers shuffled their hooves on the ground. "You'll be great, sis," said Buck.

"We'll miss you," Aggie added, blinking a few times.

"Me too," she whispered.

She quickly rubbed noses with her family and held back her tears. If she did make it up the rainbow, she wouldn't see her family for a long time. They'd never been apart, not even for one day. "Wish me luck."

"You don't need luck," her dad said. "You're kind. You're smart. You're a hard worker. You're wonderful even without magic. Believe in yourself and you'll be fine."

But Daisy didn't agree. If she didn't have magic, she would let everyone down. She slowly walked over to the end of the line behind the other ponies waiting to climb up to the school beyond the clouds. Would she be able to join them?

# Chapter Two

A pure-silver unipony stepped to the front of the crowd, standing at the base of the rainbow. Her long horn was pearly white.

"I'd like to welcome this year's class of Glitter Ponies on this gathering day. I am Headmistress Valincia. We are so pleased to continue our important tradition of teaching our treasured Glitter Ponies the ways of magic so that they may assist the royal families in the hundred kingdoms."

The group of twenty Glitter Ponies whinnied and stomped with excitement.

Daisy's heart clip-clopped in her chest. She couldn't believe this day was really here.

Headmistress Valincia continued. "As you know, the magic that was once strong in this land was nearly destroyed during the Age of Recklessness, when magic was used irresponsibly. It is our duty to see that you ponies learn the proper ways to use your

powers for the greater good. We must prepare for the day when powerful magic returns."

Daisy shivered, remembering the stories she'd read. Of magical beings thinking only of themselves. Someone casting a rain spell for their crops at the same time someone else cast a spell for dry weather. Careless spells

like that clashed, and eventually the magic weakened and faded. The dragons fled during that time. Other magical creatures simply vanished. Many ponies thought these tales were merely legends. But Daisy believed. There were misty, mysterious lands hidden throughout the world that could hold any number of secrets.

Headmistress Valincia continued. "That magic lives on in a select few horses. And we are honoured to welcome those ponies today to the Enchanted Pony Academy, hidden beyond the clouds at the other end of the rainbow. It is with great pleasure that I invite you to take your first steps on this exciting journey."

Daisy glanced over her shoulder at her parents and brothers, standing in a circle of other horse families saying goodbye to their children. She blinked back a tear and bobbed her head at them. They did the same.

A sleek unipony with a purple mane was the first to step forward. A set of stairs appeared in the rainbow and she dashed up. The crowd cheered. "Go, Violet!"

Next was a lovely pegapony, flapping her white wings. She flew the short distance to the rainbow, then walked gracefully up the colourful arch.

"We love you, Skydancer!" shouted a group of white ponies.

Skydancer looked back, fluttering her bright blue eyes. She tossed her head, and her curly, ice-blue and white mane bounced as she galloped the rest of the way into the clouds.

Daisy closed her eyes, imagining the incredible castle that awaited. The one she'd studied so many times in her books. She was moments away from seeing it. *Hopefully*, she thought.

A yellow pony with a bronze mane and matching sparkly hooves trotted back and forth in front of the rainbow. She left behind a swirl of bronze glitter.

"Goodbye, Sunny!" shouted several ponies below.

Daisy swallowed nervously. All these ponies seemed so different from her – so amazing, so confident.

The crowd cheered as the next pony approached. He was huge, with giant wings, a horn, and black sparkly hooves. Daisy didn't know one pony could have so many magical qualities.

"An allapony," someone whispered.

"Duke, Duke, Duke," some of the horses chanted, as he reared on his big hind legs.

One after the other, the ponies climbed

the rainbow. None of them seemed nervous like Daisy was. Soon, there was only one pony left before her, a midnight-blue unipony. The pony looked back at her. "See you up there!" Then she dashed over to the rainbow and climbed the stairs.

Daisy's heart was racing. It was her turn and everyone was watching. What if the stairs didn't appear? She'd be so embarrassed. She was frozen for a moment, uncertain that she could really do this. But after taking a deep breath, she slowly walked to the rainbow.

She glanced back at her parents and their big smiles. "Daisy, we love you!" Mother called.

Daisy lifted her hoof and, holding her breath, she set it on the rainbow. Her heart raced like she'd been galloping for miles. Then – she felt something solid beneath her

hoof. It was a stair! She must be magical! She took another step. She was doing it! She was climbing the rainbow! Laughing, she charged up the colourful stairs.

Below, someone gasped. "Where's her glitter?"

"Why aren't her sparkly hooves making glitter?" another pony asked.

Daisy sighed. She'd been secretly hoping if she made it up the stairs, the rainbow might activate her glitter – if she had any. Disappointed, Daisy quickly ran the rest of the way up the rainbow and into the clouds, still not convinced she belonged there.

# Chapter Three

As Daisy walked down the other side of the rainbow, the amazing castle she'd dreamed about so many times suddenly appeared.

"It's incredible!" she whispered. Tall turrets rose on each of the four corners, and a courtyard bloomed with flowers inside the walls of the castle. Orchards and fields lined the land around the magnificent school. "I'm really here!" She shivered with excitement.

The other Glitter Ponies were gathered in front of a small stage. Daisy trotted over and hid herself in the crowd before anyone could notice how plain she was. Next to her stood the lovely white pegapony she'd seen earlier.

The pegapony smiled at her. "Hi, I'm Skydancer. We didn't meet earlier. What's your name?"

"I'm Daisy. I don't know anyone here."

"Well, now we know each other, right?"

"Right," Daisy replied with a smile.

A midnight-blue unipony with a rainbow mane looked over her shoulder. "Shhhh! The welcome ceremony is starting!" She stomped her shimmery left hoof, which lit up and glowed along with her other hooves and her horn.

An orange pony with a green mane tied into a row of buns narrowed her eyes. "Electra, calm down!"

"Sorry, but I'm excited, Razzle!" Electra

said, shaking her mane. "We sailed across three oceans, and now we're finally at the Enchanted Pony Academy."

Daisy couldn't believe all the ponies' brilliant colours and sparkles. She felt completely boring with her simple pink coat and dull white mane.

All the chatter stopped when a huge horse climbed the stage. He had three horns in a triangular shape that met at the tips: one silver, one gold, one iridescent. He was big, shimmering grey, and a little scary. Daisy couldn't stop staring. In all her reading, she'd never heard of horses with three horns!

"He's a tripony," Skydancer whispered. "They're very rare."

"Good afternoon," the tripony said, his slow, deep voice booming. "I am Headmaster Elegius. Welcome to the Enchanted Pony Academy. Today is one of the most important days of your life, second only to the selection ceremony. That's when

you will be chosen by a royal child to be their loyal pet."

"I wonder who will pick me," Skydancer said dreamily.

*I wonder if* anyone *will pick me*, Daisy thought sadly.

Headmaster Elegius continued. "Testing begins tomorrow to assess your Glitter Gifts so we can place you in the right study group: pageantry, guardianship, tricks or healing. These are the skills the princes and princesses most desire in their royal pet. Our upper-year ponies will escort you to the school entrance. Then Headmistress Valincia will take you on a tour and show you to your rooms. We're so happy to have you here."

The most beautiful pony Daisy had ever seen walked over to her group. She wore a headdress with a bright-green, heart-shaped rock nestled on her forehead. Daisy knew from her books that this was heart ore, a stone found only in the deepest forests of the land. It was very hard to find.

"I'm Belissima, a second-year student,"

the pony said. She even had a gorgeous voice! "I'm lead pony of the Earth barn. Follow me and let me know if you have any questions."

The ponies had lots of questions: "What's your study group?" "What's your Glitter Gift?" "How did you get so pretty?"

Belissima let out a soft, tinkly laugh. "Let's see, my group is pageantry. And this is my skill." She closed her eyes, and her coat turned from a soft purple to a dark, sparkly purple. Her hot-pink and white mane turned to sparkly white and light purple.

"Wow," said the ponies.

Belissima flicked her tail as if to say *no big deal*. "That blue unipony over there leading the other group? That's Ranger, the head pony for the Water barn. He can make it rain. He's in the tricks group. And the purple pegapony over there, Lavender, can make flowers bloom. She's in healing."

"How is that healing?" Skydancer asked.

"Healing isn't just about making creatures better. It's healing the environment, too. Fixing burnt fields or dirty water," Belissima explained. "Some of the royal children want a pony who can help the sick people in their kingdom, and keep the environment healthy and safe." She started walking toward the school, and the group of ponies followed.

"What's pageantry for?" Daisy asked.

Belissima kicked a rock along the path. "Sometimes the children want a royal pony for ceremonial purposes, for parades and parties. They just want a pet who can put on a good show, and be exquisite and elegant."

The ponies strolled past orchards of apples as they chatted.

"And tricks?" Razzle asked. "What about tricks? That sounds fun."

Belissima laughed. "It is. The princes and princesses often like to have a pony who can entertain them and bring cheer to the people of their land."

"But guardianship is the best, isn't it?" Electra asked.

"There's value in all the study groups. But the ponies in guardianship often have the finest skills. They provide protection and guidance to their owners. Those children destined to be kings and queens usually choose a royal pet with guardianship skills to help rule their kingdoms."

Daisy couldn't decide which group she'd want to be in. They all sounded so wonderful.

They stopped at the gates to the school. Headmistress Valincia was waiting for them.

"Hello, hello. So nice to see you all. Are you ready to explore the academy?"

"Yes!" shouted the ponies, a few rearing on their back legs.

"This way." Headmistress Valincia opened the enormous front doors and led them through a courtyard into a beautiful room. It had pillars, high ceilings, and a chandelier hanging over a bubbling fountain. Giant paintings covered the walls, along with a huge map of the school grounds.

Some of the ponies "Ahhed" and some of them "Ooohed". It was the fanciest place Daisy had ever seen.

"Here's the gathering room," Headmistress Valincia said. "We host parties and important meetings here. And ahead on the right is the banquet hall."

The ponies followed her to a big room filled with long, wooden tables. Troughs

along the walls overflowed with wonderful food. "We enjoy breakfast, lunch and dinner here," the headmistress said.

The headmistress showed them the classrooms inside the academy, and then the outdoor areas for subjects like flying and weather spells. Finally, she took them to see their stables.

"There are four barns: Water, Sun, Earth,

Sky. The four elements, which bring balance to our world. Each barn has a lead pony in charge. You must follow their orders."

Then she read off the stable assignments. When she nodded at Daisy and announced that she was in the Earth barn, Daisy thought she might be getting more magical already. Not only was Belissima the lead pony of Earth, but Skydancer would be living there, too.

Daisy, Skydancer and three other new ponies followed Belissima to a big green barn.

"We've got the best barn and we have the most fun," Belissima told them. "We usually win most of the contests with the other barns, too. But there are rules to follow."

She explained how they each would have chores to keep the big main room looking nice. Everyone had to be in their stalls to sleep by nine. And they weren't to leave the school grounds.

"Will we get an incredible headdress like yours?" Skydancer asked.

Belissima laughed. "Only the lead ponies wear the headdresses. Each barn has a different stone that represents their element. Mine is heart ore, for the earth."

"What are the other stones?" a unipony asked.

"The lead pony for the Water barn has a fathom pearl, a dark blue pearl harvested from the depths of the oceans by mermaids," Belissima explained.

A few ponies gasped.

"And the Sun barn has the sunburst gem that falls from the sky during sun storms. They're very rare," Belissima said, her eyes wide.

"And what about Sky?" another pony asked.

Belissima thought for a moment. "I can't remember."

Daisy cleared her throat. "It's the sky stone. They're rainbow coloured. They grow on the ground and they can only be collected when a rainbow appears."

"That's right," Belissima said. "Very impressive."

"Thanks," Daisy whispered.

"You'll each be sharing stalls with another pony. Daisy, you're with Skydancer." Belissima opened the door to a large stall that looked like a beautiful spot in the forest. Grass covered the floor and trees lined the walls. There were two big bed cushions on the floor.

It was so wonderful that Daisy's jaw dropped.

Belissima giggled. "It's charmed to look

like the forest. We've also got stables that look like a meadow, a field and a rocky glen."

Skydancer and Daisy went into their stall. "I love this!" Skydancer said. Daisy was too stunned to say anything.

Belissima smiled as she stepped out of the room. "See you two at dinner in an hour."

Daisy and Skydancer inspected every inch of their stall. "This is so exciting. I can't wait for our tests tomorrow," Skydancer said.

Daisy looked down. In all the excitement, she'd forgotten her worries.

"What's wrong?" Skydancer asked.

"I don't know my Glitter Gift yet. Do you know yours?"

Skydancer nodded. "I can talk to any animal that has wings."

"That's so cool!" Daisy said.

Skydancer smiled. "It's lots of fun when

I'm flying. I talk to the birds going by."

Daisy wondered again about her gift. Would it be something wonderful like talking to birds? Or would it be something boring like making grass grow faster? Not all gifts were exciting. But she'd still feel better if she knew hers.

"You'll be fine," Skydancer said. "Don't worry about tomorrow."

Daisy forced a smile and nodded.

But even after a delicious dinner of carrots and hay, Daisy did worry – all night long. Dad said working hard and believing in herself was enough, but if she wanted to be a royal pony someday, she knew she'd have to be truly special.

# Chapter Four

After breakfast, Professor Xayide was waiting for the ponies in the training field. He was no bigger than a hummingbird. He moved as fast as one, too.

"I thought all the flutterponies had disappeared during the Age of Recklessness?" Daisy asked Skydancer.

"All but one family did. Now he's the only one left. It's quite sad. He's all alone."

"That's terrible," Daisy said.

Skydancer nodded.

"All right, everyone," Professor Xayide

said in a surprisingly loud voice. "Line up if you've already found your Glitter Gift and show me what you can do!"

Most of the ponies walked over to him. But Daisy was relieved to see three other ponies stay behind with her. They looked at one another nervously.

Skydancer went first with the teacher, showing him how she could chat with a passing butterfly.

Professor Xayide nodded, impressed. "That talent could be useful in any of the arts. Take your pick."

Skydancer whinnied in delight. "I always wanted to be in guardianship."

"Then that will be your study group," the professor said. "The ability to talk to animals of the air would be very useful when helping your prince or princess oversee their kingdom."

"What exactly do guardians do?" a pony near Daisy whispered.

"They help keep their kingdom peaceful," a spotted grey unipony said. "They offer their owners guidance. They're usually the smartest, bravest ponies. They used to be on guard to warn if dragons were approaching."

Daisy gasped. She had always wanted to believe the stories, but had never been sure if they were more than myths. "So dragons are real?"

"Well, they were a long time ago. But no one has seen one in hundreds of years. I'm Stone, by the way."

"I'm Daisy. Nice to meet you. You know a lot about the academy, huh?"

"I have two older brothers who went here. They both studied guardianship. That's what I want to study, too," he said.

"Are you worried you don't know your Glitter Gift yet?" Daisy asked.

"No," Stone quickly said. "No, not at all."

They turned their attention back to the ponies showing off their skills. Duke stomped on a nearby rock and it shattered into bits. He did it with one hoof! A cloud of glitter hovered in the air, mixing with the rock dust.

"Excellent," said the teacher.

Duke puffed up his chest. "I can also touch my horn to something and it will change to whatever colour I want."

"Two gifts?" Daisy asked Stone.

"It's rare, but sometimes it happens," said Stone, sounding a little annoyed.

Professor Xayide zipped around in a

circle, excited. "Very good, Duke. Those will be wonderful for the tricks group."

Duke frowned. "But I want to be a guardian."

"You'll all study basic guardian skills, but I believe your gifts are best suited for concentrating on tricks," the professor said.

Duke stalked back to the group, pawing angrily at the ground.

Two more ponies showed off their skills. Electra's horn and hooves could glow in the dark, and Razzle could copy any sound she heard. They were both placed in the tricks group, too.

"After a short break for lunch in the orchard, we're going to put you all through some tests," the professor said. "Hopefully, we'll help the remaining ponies discover what they can do. And sometimes, a pony will find they have a second gift, like Duke has."

Apples filled the nearby orchard, and Skydancer and Daisy galloped over with the other ponies to pick a few to eat.

"You won't believe what I heard from a bird nesting in a tree," Skydancer said in between bites of her juicy red fruit. "There's a river just beyond the school grounds that leads to the ocean. Seaponies live there!"

"Seaponies?" Daisy asked. She hadn't read about them in her books.

Skydancer nodded. "They live underwater. They don't have legs – just a fish tail and fins! A few of us are going to check it out. Want to come?"

"Are we allowed to? It's off school grounds," Daisy pointed out.

"It's only a little off school grounds," Skydancer said. "You can decide later. We're going after dinner."

Daisy wasn't sure what to do. She'd love to see a seapony, but she didn't want to get in trouble. After eating a few apples, they trotted back to the training field. For a moment, she'd forgotten how nervous she was.

Professor Xayide hovered in the air and waited for them. "Time to get back to work."

Back on the field, he put the ponies through all sorts of tests. They ran and stomped their hooves in different patterns, hoping to unleash their magic. To her relief, no one said anything about Daisy's hooves not making glitter.

Then Daisy spotted the headmaster and headmistress standing on the edge of the field, watching. They were looking right at her. Were they frowning, she wondered? She felt nervous until they headed back to the school.

Next the ponies practiced leaping. Rose, a pink pony who didn't know her Glitter Gift yet, flew through the air even though she didn't have wings. Everyone cheered.

"I never knew I could do that!" Rose said.

"That's an excellent skill for pageantry or guardianship," the professor said.

"I pick pageantry," she announced.

After testing the ponies to see if anyone else could fly, they took a break. Skydancer galloped over to Daisy. "Did you see what Rose did?"

"Yes," Daisy grumbled. She'd been working her tail off all afternoon, and not only were her hooves stubbornly glitter-less, she still seemed to be a totally ordinary pony.

When they were done for the day, Headmaster Elegius appeared out of nowhere with a whoosh. A greyish orb faded around him.

"He just teleported!" Skydancer whispered. "That's incredibly advanced magic!"

He walked toward Daisy. Her heart was beating fast.

"Daisy, could you please see me in my office immediately?" the headmaster asked.

"Of course," she said quietly.

Then he disappeared.

"I'm sure everything's fine," Skydancer said. But her eyes were big and round.

Daisy trudged to the headmaster's office in one of the high towers. Maybe he had been so disappointed with her performance today he was going to send her home. Maybe he'd noticed that her hooves didn't make glitter.

As she climbed the tower stairs, she paused to look out a window across the school grounds. She could see the training fields, the orchards, and beyond. Then she noticed light glinting off a river. "That's probably where the seaponies live."

She'd hate to leave such a wonderful place. But that must be why she was being called to the headmaster's office, right? To be sent home?

When she got to the top of the tower, the headmaster's door was open. "Come in," he commanded.

Daisy walked in and stood in front of his desk. She didn't dare look in his eyes.

"Are you enjoying the school so far?" he asked.

"Oh yes. I love it here."

"And you're still waiting to find your Glitter Gift."

"Yes," she said sadly.

The headmaster looked out the window behind his desk. "When I first came here, I didn't know mine."

"You didn't?"

He shook his head. His three horns sparkled in the sun streaming through the window. "It took a year before it appeared."

"What was it?"

He laughed. "I can run backward faster than I run forward."

"That's interesting," Daisy said politely.

"But it's not helpful for much. They put me in tricks because they didn't know what else to do with me. Yet here I am, headmaster of the academy. How could I manage that if I can only run backward fast?"

"I don't know," Daisy said.

"Because I trained harder at everything than all the other students. I learned whatever I could from anyone willing to teach me."

She could do that, couldn't she? She took a deep breath. "Have you ever had a student who never found their Glitter Gift?"

"No," he said, looking her straight in the eye.

She swallowed nervously. "But Headmaster Elegius, my hooves don't make glitter."

"I know."

"It's possible I might not be able to do magic at all."

"I'd be very surprised if that were true. If your hooves don't make glitter, there must be a good reason why. And you'll figure that out someday. I know you will."

She nodded.

"For now, I want you to work your hardest. Follow the rules. And while you wait to discover your gift, just believe in yourself. Do you understand?"

"I do, sir." But she *didn't* know what he meant. Why would she believe in her boring old self? It reminded her of what her father had told her before she climbed the rainbow.

"Good. Now head back to your stable and clean up for dinner."

"Thank you, sir." She galloped down the stairs, and paused again to look out the window. No way would she be joining the other ponies on their adventure to spy on the seaponies. She'd promised the headmaster she'd follow the rules.

# Chapter Five

Daisy hurried to the banquet hall for dinner. She took a few carrots from the trough and a scoop of oats. There was even a dish of sugar cubes with a lever that released a few into her bucket. What a treat!

She carried her bucket over to the table where Skydancer, Electra and Razzle stood.

"Is everything OK?" Skydancer asked.

"The headmaster just wanted to tell me to keep working hard."

Skydancer smiled at her. "See? I told you not to worry."

The ponies munched and crunched. Daisy thought she'd never tasted better food. She glanced over at Duke's table, where he was changing the colour of his friends' apples with a touch of his horn. She wondered if a purple apple tasted different from a red one.

"Are you guys ready to find the seaponies?" Razzle asked. "A bunch of other ponies want to come, too. We're meeting outside the stables in half an hour."

Daisy pushed away the rest of her food. "I don't want to get in trouble by leaving the grounds."

"Rules are for fools," Razzle said. "No one will know."

Maybe not, but she wasn't going to risk it. She'd made a promise to the headmaster. "Sorry. You guys will have to tell me what the seaponies look like." Daisy walked out of the cafeteria while the rest of the ponies plotted their adventure.

She stopped in the great hall and looked at the beautiful decorations.

She inspected the map of the grounds. She'd been wanting to take a closer look. The maps she'd seen in her library books hadn't been so detailed. There was still so much to learn about this place. That was one thing she could do well – read, study, learn. The thought comforted her.

On the map, she saw the river from the sea twisted down from the North and came close to the forest beyond the orchard. An X marked that spot identifying it. She remembered seeing the river out of the tower window. The ponies wouldn't be far from the campus, but they would have to leave it to see the seaponies.

Then Daisy noticed something. She took a step closer and followed the course of the river. Once it left the forest, it went back up and around the school, and it came near the faraway forest on the other side of the flying field. That was on school grounds. There was a way to see the seaponies without leaving school property. It just wasn't marked with an X.

She raced off to meet the other ponies and tell them her news. They were leaving the stables when she found them.

"Hey, everyone, stop!"

"Daisy, don't worry," Skydancer said. "We're not going to get in trouble. No one's going to see us."

"I found a way to look at the river without leaving school grounds. There's another spot where the river comes through the forest. I saw it on the map in the great hall. Follow me!"

Daisy led the ponies across the orchard to a small forest.

Skydancer paused. "It's really dark in there. Maybe this wasn't a good idea."

"Don't be scared." Electra lit up her horn so they could see in the shadowy woods.

"That's much better," Skydancer said, cautiously following Daisy.

After a while, Skydancer stopped to ask a butterfly if they were getting close. The butterfly informed her they were almost there.

They walked along some more, then paused.

"I can hear the river!" Daisy cried.

The ponies galloped after her until they came to a wide, blue river sparkling in the setting sun.

"It's beautiful!" Razzle said.

"Where are the seaponies?" Skydancer asked.

"Don't they live underwater?" Daisy asked. "How are we supposed to see them?"

"Someone told me they come up if they hear music," Electra said.

"Really?" Daisy asked.

"We have to sing," Electra said. She started singing a song, but before she'd got through the first verse, all the other ponies were pressing their ears flat.

"They'll never come up if they hear that!" Skydancer said.

Electra stuck her nose in the air, offended. But she stopped singing.

"Let me try," Daisy said. "My mother used to sing me to sleep. I remember all her songs." Daisy closed her eyes and started to sing. *"Wind in the willows, moon in the sky, sleep my little pony, while I sing this lullaby."*

The ponies were silent. Did they think she was horrible? "Maybe I don't do it as well as my mother," Daisy said.

"No," Skydancer said. "That was amazing."

"Look!" Razzle said, pointing her hoof toward the river.

A few slick heads popped up from the surface of the water. Their snouts were long and their ears were small. Bits of shell and coral were threaded in their manes.

"Seaponies!" Skydancer squealed. "You did it, Daisy!"

The seaponies blinked at them with big, dark eyes, then skittered back underwater. They flashed their tails as they dived into the river.

The ponies ran back to the school, laughing and whinnying as they went. "That was so cool!" Razzle said.

Electra charged ahead of the group,

lighting up her horn and hooves as she raced across the field. "Woo-hoo!"

Daisy was glad she'd helped them find the seaponies.

When they got back to the stables, they went to their stalls right before nine and fell fast asleep.

The next morning after breakfast, the new ponies returned to the training fields again. Headmaster Elegius was standing there. Daisy's heart started beating fast.

He stepped forward. "Daisy, can you come here please?"

She walked over to him while all the other ponies stood silently watching. She felt very nervous.

"I understand you led a group to find

the seaponies last night," he said.

She took a step back. "How did you know?"

"I have many animals in the forest and the grounds who keep track of my students. They report everything to me. So, is it true?"

Looking down, Daisy nodded. "We wanted to see if the seaponies were real."

"And?" he asked.

"They are," Daisy said, certain she was about to get in trouble – in front of everyone.

"Daisy found a place to see them without leaving the school grounds," Skydancer explained.

"And she sang to them and they came up to the top of the water!" Razzle added.

"I know. My animal caretakers told me," the headmaster said.

"Really?" Skydancer asked.

"I have eyes and ears everywhere," he said.

"Are you mad, sir?" Daisy asked.

He smiled. "Not at all. Students from every new class want to catch a glimpse of the seaponies, and they usually try to leave school grounds to do it. However, they are always stopped by my caretakers before they do. But you, Daisy, you found the spot where you could observe them without leaving the grounds. And you got them to rise. You have to be special to do that." He winked at her.

"Thank you, sir," she said softly. Even if she wasn't in trouble, it was embarrassing to be the centre of attention!

"Now everyone, back to your studies," Headmaster Elegius said. "The royal children will be touring the school in a few weeks."

The ponies scampered over to the group of students on the field, but Daisy hung back. The headmaster's announcement was a surprise. She never imagined she'd see the royal children so soon. Would she know her Glitter Gift by then?

"Come on, Daisy!" Skydancer shouted.

Daisy trotted over to join the others.

After going through more tests and drills, another one of the ponies discovered he could lift water out of a puddle and swirl it around with his horn. It was a neat gift, but now, it was just Daisy and Stone waiting to discover what they could do. Stone didn't look any happier than Daisy felt.

# Chapter Six

"Ponies, now that most of you have discovered your Glitter Gifts, it is time to work on basic magic," said Professor Zeldini at the beginning of classes the next week. "The most useful spell you can master is the art of levitation. With this skill, you can manipulate pens to write, needles to sew, and so on. Thus, it is the first we shall study."

Daisy gulped. How was she supposed to do that?

"Let's start by levitating our Ever Ink

quills. You each get one of your very own,
which you will someday store in your saddle."
Professor Zeldini handed a beautiful feather
to each student. "Be careful with these, they
are precious. Our Inky Quillcocks drop
their feathers just once in their lifetime. That
is our only opportunity to collect these quills
that never run out of ink."

Daisy stared at the marvellous feather
lying on the ground in front of her. She was

supposed to levitate it? Besides climbing the rainbow stairs, she hadn't done one magical thing since arriving at the academy.

"If you haven't already figured it out," the professor said, "Glitter Ponies activate their magic by stomping the ground. That's why you create trails of sparkles when you run."

Daisy hung her head, certain everyone was staring at her.

"So first we activate our magic, then we concentrate very hard on the spell we wish to cast. We have to focus, and believe strongly that we can do it. In this case, we will focus on the thing we wish to levitate. Sometimes chanting a rhyme will help. Ready? Stomp your hooves, then say, *I know I will – raise this quill – day or night – so I may write.*"

All around Daisy, ponies were stomping their hooves and repeating the rhyme. She was just gathering the courage to try.

Skydancer's quill shot up into the air. She laughed. "Aren't you going to do it?" she asked Daisy.

"Of course." Daisy pawed at the ground and whispered the chant. *"I know I will – raise this quill – day or night – so I may write."* Slowly the feather started to shake and rose a few inches from the ground before falling back.

"Well, it was just your first try," Skydancer said, as she zoomed her quill through the air like it was a bird.

Daisy blinked at the feather. There was some magic in her after all!

*But not very much*, she thought sadly.

"Give it another go," Professor Zeldini said, stepping closer to Daisy.

Daisy stomped her hooves and repeated the chant. *"I know I will – raise this quill – day or night – so I may write."*

The quill rose more quickly this time,

but she certainly didn't feel like she had control over it.

"I'm not good at this," Daisy said.

"Now, now. It's a start," Professor Zeldini said. "I want you to practise and *believe* you can do it."

Just then, sparks flew across the room.

"What ever is going on?" Professor Zeldini asked.

"I don't know!" Stone shouted. "They started shooting out of my horn!"

"It must be your Glitter Gift!" Electra shouted.

Stone fired a long stream of sparks into the air, laughing.

The other ponies gathered around Stone and cheered. Daisy forced a smile. She was now the only pony at the academy who didn't know her Glitter Gift.

If she even had one.

# Chapter Seven

That week was filled with new classes. Professor Mortimer worked with the ponies on weather skills. "The ponies most skilled at weather casting can summon a rainbow, which as you know strengthens our magic."

So far, Daisy was only able to stir a weak breeze. Duke managed to create a swirl of snow on his first try.

"All these classes are a lot harder than I thought," Daisy told Skydancer.

Skydancer rustled her wings. "It's challenging, but I'm having fun, aren't you?"

*It would be a whole lot more fun if I was better at this*, Daisy thought.

Next it was off to pageantry. The ponies had to learn basic skills in all the study groups. *Luckily, prancing prettily doesn't require magic*, Daisy thought as they strutted around the track on the training field.

But then in tricks class, she had to try casting spells to make items appear.

No matter how many times she said,

"*Right here — make a flower appear,*" it just wouldn't work. Duke managed to get a sugar cube to show up. Which he gobbled up with a smile.

When classes were over, it was a huge relief to finally go to lunch, a place where she didn't need magic.

The ponies who knew their Glitter Gifts spent an extra hour after classes focusing on their area of study. That meant Daisy had a free hour to use however she wanted.

So Daisy nosed around the library, where she discovered books on the history of the academy that she'd never seen at home. There was so much more to learn! She discovered the seaponies had an academy underwater, to train for the day they are matched with their mer-princes and princesses. "Cool!" she whispered to herself.

Excited, she raced to the river, singing to the

seaponies who occasionally popped their heads above the water to listen. Then she relaxed under a tree, studying more new books.

She read about other magical creatures that disappeared after the Age of Recklessness, the horses and dragonflies even tinier than Professor Xayide, who hadn't been seen since. Her head spun with this exciting new information.

The next day during her spare hour,

Daisy made her way down to the kitchens. The head pony chef was going out to pick apples from the orchard.

"Can I help you?" Daisy asked.

"Sure," the pony chef said.

They walked to the orchard, where the trees were full of fruit. "You want to pick the ones on the outside of the tree. Those ripen first," the chef explained.

Daisy quickly filled a bucket with apples and shared them with her friends after they finished class.

"These are so good!" Razzle said. "So sweet!"

"Today I learned the apples on the outside of the tree ripen first," Daisy told them.

"Cool, I didn't know that," Electra said. Daisy felt good teaching her friends something new.

The next day, she visited the healing

room and observed how those ponies used healing magic.

"I see you're learning all about our school," Headmistress Valincia said when she saw Daisy returning to her stable.

"It's all so interesting," Daisy said. "Did you know they use lavender to clean wounds?"

"I did know that. But most of the students don't. I'm impressed, Daisy."

Daisy blushed and looked down. She felt a bit better about everything.

But when Skydancer got back from class, she had terrible news.

"Did you hear? The princes and princesses will be coming sooner than we thought! They want to see our new class of ponies. We have to put together a special routine!"

"Really?" Daisy gulped. "They're going to watch what we can do?"

"Yes! The professors will enchant the

rainbow so the children can climb through the clouds to visit the school. Isn't that exciting? We get to show off our magic. I can't wait!" She flapped her wings and twirled in the air.

Magic? In front of everyone? Daisy had learned some very basic magic spells, but nothing impressive. What was she going to do for her routine?

# Chapter Eight

The next day, Headmistress Valincia and Headmaster Elegius led the ponies on to the training field.

"Each of you must create a routine showcasing your best qualities," the headmistress told them. "Of course, you want to include your Glitter Gift and any other skills at which you are particularly adept."

Daisy practised and practised with her quill so she could write a greeting for the children on a scroll of paper. She tried not to pay attention to everyone else's fabulous

routines. Stone had learned to control the
sparks coming from his horn and was able
to write messages in the air. A quill writing
on paper was so boring in comparison.

The ponies spent the next few days
working on their routines. Skydancer
created a beautiful flying act that ended
with her talking to a pack of birds, then
inviting them to fly with her.

Duke galloped through an obstacle course, smashing rocks with his hooves along the way.

Daisy had no idea what she should do besides write with a quill and summon a weak breeze. It was hopeless.

"You could sing," Razzle offered. "You have a lovely voice."

Skydancer nodded. "And you could share all the interesting things you've learned about the school."

"You could tell everyone what a good friend you are by keeping us from getting in trouble," Electra said.

"Yes! We'll cheer you on when you go on the field so everyone knows how much we love you," Skydancer said.

The ponies started chanting, "Daisy! Daisy! Daisy!"

Daisy felt her cheeks warming in

embarrassment from all the attention.

Headmistress Valincia held up a hoof to quiet the group. "Daisy, I think those are wonderful ideas. You can trot on to the field and sing, cast a spell or two, and your classmates will show their love for you. Then the royal children will have no doubt how wonderful you are."

Daisy forced a smile and nodded. She was touched by how much her classmates cared for her. But it was going to be very hard being the only pony at the exhibition who didn't have a Glitter Gift to show off. And what about her hooves not making glitter? Would they notice that, too? As the rest of the ponies went back to their stables to prepare for dinner, Daisy headed to the river. She wanted to be alone.

She settled on the ground, resting her

head between her front legs, blinking back tears. But the tears kept coming stronger, and soon she was sobbing.

"What's wrong?" a soft voice asked.

Daisy looked up, astonished to see a seapony staring at her. "I didn't know you guys could talk."

The pony nodded her head. "We're usually shy around creatures from above, but your sad crying called me to the surface.

Is there anything I can do to help? I'm Marina."

"I'm Daisy, and I'm the only pony at the academy who doesn't know their Glitter Gift yet. I'm pretty sure I don't have one. And soon we have a big exposition with the royal children to show what we can do, and I can't do much of anything." She sniffed.

"Oh," Marina said sympathetically. "It took a long time for me to find my Sea Savvy. But one day, I discovered I could change colours to blend in with the background."

"That's amazing," Daisy said.

Marina smiled. "You'll find your Glitter Gift. You just have to believe in yourself."

Daisy tried not to groan. Everyone kept telling her that but so far, it hadn't worked.

"Good luck, Daisy. Everything will be

fine. You're the first Glitter Pony I've ever talked to. You're special to me."

"Thanks, Marina."

Marina smiled, then disappeared beneath the water.

Feeling better, Daisy trotted back to her stable. She believed in herself, didn't she?

# Chapter Nine

The morning the royal children were scheduled to visit, the ponies bathed in the river. "We have to look our best!" Electra said.

Belissima frowned. "It's not the only important thing. You have to show your best magic, and be friendly, too."

Electra turned to Skydancer and Daisy. "Easy for her to say," she muttered. "Belissima always looks perfect!"

Suddenly, a dark head rose from the surface and Marina swam over to Daisy, presenting her with a crown of seashells and coral.

"It's so pretty!" Daisy dipped her head so Marina could place the crown on her. "Thank you!"

Marina nodded and slipped back under the water.

"Wow! That's gorgeous. She really likes you!" Skydancer said.

"I've been singing to them while everyone else has been working on their Glitter Gifts." She didn't tell her how Marina had found her crying by the riverbank.

"You'll be the only one out there with a crown," Skydancer said.

That made Daisy feel a little better.

When they dried off, Skydancer asked a few birds in a nearby tree to thread daisies into her mane. The birds flew away and returned with flowers clutched in their beaks. Bobbing through the air, they tucked the posies in her beautiful blue and white mane.

Daisy smiled at her friend. "You look magical."

"How about some braids?" Skydancer asked.

Daisy nodded excitedly, and three birds flew over, each grabbing tiny sections of her mane. They crossed them back and forth until she had several delicate braids falling along her neck.

"Thank you!" she cried. Maybe her splendid mane and seapony crown would distract the royal children from noticing that she didn't have a Glitter Gift. Or that her hooves didn't make glitter.

Maybe she should hide in her stable instead.

After a breakfast of oats and apples, the ponies lined up in the arena. Even the second-year ponies were there. Daisy hadn't been in the huge ring before. It was amazing. Stands for the children and their

families circled the field. Tall flags from each of the kingdoms lined the stadium, flapping in the breeze.

But when the princes and princesses started filing into the arena, Daisy's stomach felt hollow.

"I'm nervous," Skydancer said.

"Me too," Belissima said. "I'll be part

of the next selection class. One of these children will choose me."

Once the arena was filled, the headmaster and headmistress climbed on to the stage behind the ponies.

"Welcome, princes and princesses of the hundred kingdoms," Headmistress Valincia said. "Our ponies have been working hard and are delighted to show you their magic and their talents today. First up, the second-year students, who will be part of our selection ceremonies this year. Then you'll meet our newest ponies, who will be matched with their owners next year. Sit back and enjoy the show!"

Belissima trotted into the arena. Girls in the crowd stood to get a better look at her beauty. She pranced across the field, but Daisy could see she wasn't smiling. Then she stopped in the middle and paused, before her coat turned from light purple to dark purple. She got a big round of applause from the crowd. Lots of girls shrieked that they were going to choose her for their pet.

"I think I'm going to throw up!" Skydancer whispered, shuffling her feet.

"Why?" Daisy asked. "Your routine is awesome. You'll do great."

Skydancer blew out a long breath. "Thanks. You're such a good friend."

The rest of the second-year ponies performed, and they all got plenty of cheers from the princes and princesses.

Then it was time for the first-year ponies. Duke trotted out first and the crowd went wild as he stomped the huge boulders into dust. They gasped when he touched one of the rocks with his horn and turned it red before he destroyed it.

After Duke, Razzle galloped on to the field, leaving a cloud of green glitter behind her. A few animals from the stables joined her, and she copied the sounds of the chickens, the cows and the ducks. Everyone enjoyed her mimicking.

Daisy was the last pony on the list and she was getting more nervous as the line grew shorter. What if no one clapped? What if people booed her? What if they laughed?

Skydancer's routine was Daisy's favourite. Her friend got a standing ovation when she finally landed on the ground with her bird friends perched on her wings.

Then Daisy heard her own name announced.

"Our final presentation is from one of our most wonderful students," Headmaster Elegius said. "Let's give a warm welcome to Daisy!"

Daisy pranced on to the field as she'd practised. She did a simple spell to make her quill write "Hello children" on a large scroll floating next to her. Then she stopped to sing in the middle of the field. That got a polite round of applause. It wasn't the most exciting routine, but it was finally over. She bowed and galloped toward the rest of the ponies as they chanted, "Daisy, Daisy, Daisy!"

Then she heard whispers from the crowd. "Where is her glitter?"

"Why aren't her hooves making glitter?"

This was horrible. She should have stayed in her stable instead of embarrassing herself. She closed her eyes, wishing with all her might that she could disappear. *"I don't want to be here, please let me disappear!"* she whispered to herself.

Then the crowd gasped. "Where did she go?"

"I can't see her!" someone said.

"That pony vanished!" another person cried.

Daisy looked over at her classmates. They all looked shocked, too.

"Daisy, where did you go?" Skydancer asked, looking around.

She ran back to the centre of the field, but people in the arena were still standing, looking for her.

Daisy lifted her hoof. She couldn't see it, either! How did that happen? *I wished in a rhyme*, Daisy realized. *And I really, really wanted to disappear!*

She stopped running and closed her eyes again. *I wish my friends could see me again*, she thought. Not quite a rhyme but maybe close enough?

Then the crowd roared. "What an incredible Glitter Gift!" someone cried from the crowd. "She can turn invisible!"

"That's the pony I want to choose," a little girl said.

"*I'm* going to pick that pony next year," said another child.

"No, I am!" shouted a boy.

Her friends started chanting once more. "Daisy! Daisy! Daisy!"

Daisy wasn't sure she could make it happen again. So she closed her eyes and wished again she could disappear. And she did!

The crowd gasped.

Daisy trotted over to her classmates and wished she could reappear. The crowd cheered when she became visible once more among her friends.

Skydancer nudged Daisy with her nose. "See? I told you that you'd have a wonderful Glitter Gift."

"I can't believe it," Daisy said, breathless.

Her magic wasn't weak, after all! For fun, she tried levitating a rock nearby. If she could turn invisible, certainly she could raise a rock, right?

She stomped the ground and thought to herself, *That rock over there, fly into the air!*

The rock shot up off the ground.

Daisy laughed and reared her front legs. *I just had to really want to do it. I had to believe I could do it.*

After Headmaster Elegius invited the children to come down to the field and visit with the ponies, he walked over to her with a huge grin.

"Congratulations, that's a fine gift. One we've never seen before at the academy."

"Really?" asked Daisy.

"Really. And now we know why your hooves don't make glitter. You wouldn't be invisible with a trail of glitter behind you."

Daisy's ears perked up. "That's true!"

"You'd be a perfect guardian pony,"
Headmistress Valincia said, walking over to
join them. "It's an incredible gift. It's like
the magic seen years ago. Strong magic."
She looked at the headmaster and raised an
eyebrow. He nodded thoughtfully.

"So is that going to be my study group?"
Daisy asked. "Guardianship?"

"Turning invisible would also be suitable

for tricks, but you'd be quite an asset as a guardian," the headmaster said. "It's your decision."

"If you think guardianship would be best, that's what I choose," Daisy said, a bit overwhelmed by the responsibility of helping a queen or king rule someday. But deep down, she now had no doubt she could do it.

The children rushed over to Daisy, stroking her mane and patting her back. "I'd love to have you as my pony," one little girl said. "Then I could disappear with you when it was time for school."

Daisy laughed.

"I'd sit on you and we'd disappear and I wouldn't have to be a princess for a little while," said another girl with long red braids.

"Well, I won't be in the selection ceremonies this year, but I will be next

year." Daisy's heart swelled with pride as she saw the excited faces of the children gathered around her.

Once the princes and princesses left, it was time for the celebration feast. Everyone cheered when Daisy walked into the banquet hall.

Headmaster Elegius walked up to her. "Get used to all the attention, Daisy. I hope you're feeling better now."

"Oh, I am. I only wish I could let my

family know I discovered my Glitter Gift. I had them pretty worried when I left for the academy."

"We have a day off classes tomorrow so we can clean up from today's festivities. Why don't you pay them a visit?" he asked.

"Really?"

He grinned. "Yes. You've earned it."

# Chapter Ten

The next day, Daisy trotted down the rainbow staircase and ran the entire way to her family's farm.

Her father looked up and his eyes widened. "Daisy, is everything all right?"

Daisy's mother stepped out of the barn. "Oh, sweetheart. We told you that you'd always have a place at our farm."

"So you didn't have a Glitter Gift?" her father asked quietly.

Daisy kicked up her front hooves. "No, I do! And the headmaster says he's never seen it before." Daisy closed her eyes, stomped her hooves, and wished she could disappear.

Her father gasped. "My word! That is remarkable."

"Oh, honey. That's incredible," Mother said.

Daisy closed her eyes again and wished to be seen.

Her parents cheered.

"The headmaster let me come down to tell you the great news," Daisy said. "I have to go show my brothers."

Daisy saw them grazing in the field. She wished herself invisible and quietly walked over. They both looked up, ears pricking.

"Who's there?" Buck asked.

Daisy couldn't hold back her giggle. "It's me. Daisy."

"Where are you?" Aggie asked.

Buck looked confused. "I can't see you."

"Exactly," she said, wishing herself to be seen. "I can turn invisible."

Their mouths dropped open.

She turned herself invisible again. "Turns out to be a good thing my hooves don't make glitter, don't you think?"

She trotted in front of them and reappeared. They reared up, kicking their

front legs in excitement. "That's amazing!" Buck shouted.

"I'm sorry we used to tease you so much," Aggie said, flicking his tail sadly. "We should have believed in you."

"That's OK. I didn't believe in myself, either. But now I do! Come on, let's go eat lunch."

They trotted back to the barn, where their parents had a delicious dandelion salad waiting.

After they'd eaten and Daisy had shared all her stories from school, her family walked her back to the rainbow.

"I love the academy so much," Daisy said. "I'm so glad I got to go, even though I was scared at first."

"Me too," Dad said.

"We'll miss you," Mother said.

"Don't worry. I'll write! I can levitate a quill!"

"Awesome!" Buck said.

She nudged noses with her parents, playfully flicked her brothers with her tail, then galloped to the rainbow and disappeared. She pranced up the stairs and shouted, "Thank goodness my hooves don't make glitter!"

Then she climbed through the clouds and trotted back to the Enchanted Pony Academy. She went straight to the library and took out her favourite books on the history of the school. There were certainly more secrets and facts she could learn to help her friends. Just because she'd found her Glitter Gift didn't mean she was going to stop working hard and doing her best.

And most important, believing in herself – no matter what.

# Acknowledgments

It's time for you to shout out a thank-you to my daughter Riley, because without her, you would not be reading this book. (But shout it quietly if it's bedtime!)

I hadn't planned to write chapter books or books about ponies until I was teasing her one night. She was ten years old at the time, and *loved, loved, loved* ponies. I told her that I was going to write a book about mean, grumpy ponies who don't share, and she got so mad! She told me that if I was going to write a book about ponies, they had to go to a special school and be magical and wonderful! I thought, *Hey! That sounds good to me.* (It was a great fit since I spent half of my childhood drawing pictures of unicorns and reading books about them. I still have my unicorn bed sheets from when I was little!) So Riley and I started talking and planning, and we created the fabulous world of Enchanted Pony Academy. Together, we came up with the story you just read.

Publishing a book takes a while, and Riley will be thirteen when the books come out. Maybe she's not quite so in love with ponies any more, but she is still the most fabulous, inventive, artistic, interesting child I can imagine, and I can't wait to see what she continues to create as she gets older. Riley has a very special Glitter Gift indeed. I love you, kiddo! Thanks for sharing this journey with me.

The magic continues! Read on for a
sneak peek at Skydancer's story...

Lisa Ann Scott

Enchanted
Pony Academy

Wings That Shine

# Chapter One

Skydancer rustled her wings in excitement as she listened to plans for the Homecoming celebration. It was her first month at the Enchanted Pony Academy, the magical school hidden beyond the clouds. At the academy she and the other Glitter Ponies worked on their magic to become pets for the royal children of the hundred kingdoms.

"Homecoming is our first competition between the four barns," explained Belissima, the lead pony of Skydancer's barn, Earth barn. There were four barns at the school: Earth, Sun, Sky, and Water. "Homecoming is so much fun!"

Skydancer's best friend, Daisy, swished her tail and smiled. Every pony had a Glitter Gift, but Daisy had one of the most incredible ones. She could turn invisible! And she was a wonderful friend.

"We must have the best float for the school-spirit contest," Belissima went on, pacing up and down at the front of their barn. "We'll use our magical talents to create an amazing float and then enter it in the parade around the exhibition field. Earth barn almost always wins, but we need some great ideas. Anyone have something spectacular in mind?"

"I could put on a fireworks show," said Stone, stomping his hooves. His Glitter Gift was making sparks shoot from his horn and he loved playing tricks and surprising other

ponies. "Turn my sparks into fireworks!"
A few pops fizzled from his horn.

"Your spell didn't rhyme. Of course
it didn't work!" said Lavender, making a
row of posies bloom at her feet. She loved
showing off her cool Glitter Gift. "I can
certainly provide some flowers for the
float!"

Skydancer swished her tail. "I will ask
my bird friends if they can fly along with
the float and sing." Since her Glitter Gift
was talking to other winged creatures, she

knew she could get them to help.

"Great! We have to work together to create something amazing," Belissima said. "But the student who works the hardest and contributes the most out of all the students in the four barns will be named Grand Pony Marshal of the Homecoming parade. The marshal even gets to pull the golden chariot around the track, leading the floats! All our former students will be returning to the school with their royal children for the celebration! Your families can come, too. It's a wonderful day."

The ponies started whinnying and chattering.

"And you get to wear *this*." Belissima levitated a beautiful medal in front of the group. The rare gems from each barn were embedded in a gold circle. "This medal has been worn by the Grand Pony

Marshal at Homecoming for hundreds of years. Usually, second-year ponies win that honour, but you never know! Maybe it'll be your turn next. Pass it around for a closer look at it. But be careful. It is very old and very precious."

The ponies took turns admiring the incredible piece. Skydancer could imagine it shining brightly on her chest as she pranced around the exhibition field. Her parents would be so proud! She was their only pony, and they expected big things from her. That medal would prove she was as special as they hoped she'd be. And wouldn't that be a great way to prove she'd be a perfect pet for the royal children someday? She was going to work her hardest on the float so she could be named Grand Pony Marshal.

"Let's get busy. Homecoming is in less than a week." Belissima took back the medal.

Skydancer couldn't wait to talk to her bird friends for some float ideas. Maybe she could lasso a cloud and make it look like the float was ... floating? Skydancer chuckled, amused by the funny thought.

As the ponies started leaving, Belissima stopped Skydancer. "Could you fly this back to Headmaster Elegius? He wants to put it away for safekeeping. We're lucky he even let us look at it." She gave her

the medal.

"No problem." Skydancer liked being helpful, especially here at the academy. Someday, she'd be helping her future owner, one of the royal children of the hundred kingdoms. She and the other ponies had to practise being of service.

With the medal hanging around her neck, Skydancer flew toward the castle. The headmaster's office was in one of the tall turrets. Skydancer soared through the air feeling positively majestic.

*I don't have to go straight to his office, do I?* she wondered. *I'll take it back in a little while. I'm going to enjoy this a bit longer.*

She swooped through the air over the training fields, then above the apple orchards. She had to be careful not to leave school grounds. That wasn't allowed.

She flew over the river, wondering if

she'd see one of the seaponies rising to the surface. Skydancer and her friends had ventured out to spy on them when they'd first arrived at school. Later, Daisy befriended a seapony named Marina, trading apples for their delicious seaweed that grew in great forests underwater. Marina loved hearing about the Enchanted Pony Academy and comparing it to the school the seaponies attended to become helpers for the royal mer-children.

Wouldn't Marina be impressed if Skydancer became Grand Pony Marshal? Her parents would be, too. *Everyone* would be impressed. She was only a first-year student.

She flapped her wings in the breeze, closing her eyes as she imagined the cheers she'd receive as Grand Pony Marshal.

"Skydancer! Skydancer!" everyone would

chant. She could almost hear her name ringing out across the field.

She opened her eyes. She really could hear her name being called. Several bird friends were flying alongside her trying to get her attention.

"Skydancer!" a bird called. "Stop!"

# Lisa Ann Scott

is the author of *School of Charm*. A former TV news reporter and anchor, she currently works as a voice-over artist and writer. She lives in Upstate New York with her husband and two kids. For more about Lisa and her books, visit LisaAnnScott.com.